Jon Scieszka's TRUCKTOWN

TRUCKS LINE UP

BY JON SCIESZKA

CHARACTERS AND ENVIRONMENTS DEVELOPED BY THE

dESIGN garage

DAVID SHANNON   **LOREN LONG**   **DAVID GORDON**

ILLUSTRATION CREW:

Executive Producer:

TOT
INDUSTRIES

Creative Supervisor: Nina Rappaport Brown ○ Drawings by: Dan Root ○ Color by: Antonio Reyna

Art Director: Aviva Shur

READY-TO-ROLL

SIMON SPOTLIGHT
NEW YORK   LONDON   TORONTO   SYDNEY

SIMON SPOTLIGHT
An imprint of Simon & Schuster Children's Publishing Division
1230 Avenue of the Americas, New York, NY 10020

For information about special discounts for bulk purchases, please contact Simon & Schuster Special Sales at 1-866-506-1949
or business@simonandschuster.com. Manufactured in the United States of America 0111 LAK
First Simon Spotlight edition February 2011 10 9 8 7 6 5 4 3 2 1
Library of Congress Cataloging-in-Publication Data
Scieszka, Jon.
Trucks line up / by Jon Scieszka ; artwork created by the Design Garage: David Gordon, Loren Long, David Shannon. — 1st Simon
Spotlight ed.
p. cm. — (Ready-to-read) (Jon Scieszka's Trucktown)
Summary: As soon as Jack Truck wakes up he gets the other trucks in line, but somehow he misses Pete.
[1. Trucks--Fiction] I. Design Garage. II. Title.
PZ7.S41267Tnt 2011
[E]--dc22
2009035952
ISBN 978-1-4169-4147-7 (pbk)
ISBN 978-1-4169-4158-3 (hc)

Jack wakes up.
He gives his call:
"Trucks line up!"

"Blue trucks here.
Red trucks there.

Trucks **line up!"**

"Trucks with scrapers,

trucks with flashers.

Trucks **line up!**"

"Trucks in pink.
Trucks in green.
Big Rig—any time you want.

Trucks line **up!**"

"That should do it.
Here we go."

"Hey," says Pete.
"What about me?"

"Ooops. Sorry, Pete.
Red? Blue?
Scraper? Flasher?"

"No,
no, no,
and
no."

"Um . . .
Orange with scooper,
ladder, muffler,
and a name that starts
with P?"

"Now we are ready.
Every truck.

Ready. Set. **Go!"**

Trucks go down.

Trucks go up.

Trucks go round and round and round.

Then Jack honks his horn and gives his call:

"TRUCKS ...

. . . UP!"

LINE . . .